Stain
this
pg.

MUTILATION
OFFICIALLY
NOTED

Grayslake Area Public Library District
Grayslake, Illinois

1. A fine will be charged on each book which is not returned when it is due.

2. All injuries to books beyond reasonable wear and all losses shall be made good to the satisfaction of the Librarian.

3. Each borrower is held responsible for all books drawn on his card and for all fines accruing on the same.

Rabbit's Skating Party

By Ann Staman

Illustrated by Tatjana Mai-Wyss

2

Little Mouse went to Rabbit's party.

"Come on!" said Rabbit.

"We are going to skate."

"Oh," said Little Mouse.

4

"Can you skate?" said Rabbit.

"Oh, yes," said Little Mouse.

"I can skate."

6

Little Mouse got up.

He fell down.

He got up.

He fell down.

"Come on!" shouted Rabbit.

"We are going to eat the cake."

"Here I come!"

shouted Little Mouse.

"Oh, no!"

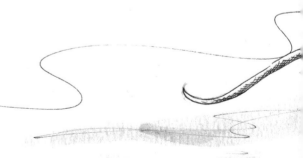

Happy Birthday Rabbit

13

Rabbit looked at

Little Mouse in the cake.

"**Can** you skate?"

said Rabbit.

"Oh, yes," said Little Mouse.

"I can **skate**, but I can't **stop**."